The New Adventures of Postman Pat

A

Postman Pat™

Postman Pat has too many parcels
Postman Pat and the big surprise
Postman Pat and the hole in the road

John Cunliffe

Illustrated by Stuart Trot

from the original television designs by **Ivor Wood**

Hodder
Children's
Books

a division of Hodder Headline plc

Postman Pat
has too many parcels

First published 1997
by Hodder Children's Books
a division of Hodder Headline plc,
338 Euston Road, London NW1 3BH

This edition first published 1998

Story copyright © 1997 Ivor Wood and John Cunliffe
Text copyright © 1997 John Cunliffe
Illustrations copyright © 1997 Hodder Children's Books
and Woodland Animations Ltd

ISBN 0 340 71629 0
10 9 8 7 6 5 4 3 2 1

Printed in Italy

It was a busy day in Greendale. Peter Fogg was dashing off to do the milking, on his motorbike, and Ted was on his way, in his lorry, to mend a hole in a roof.

Pat was out early as well, but *he* was going slowly! He had such a load of parcels today! Some of them wanted to escape. Miss Hubbard found one that had got away, lying on the ground.

"Oh - a parcel - now I wonder who . . .? Well, there's an address on it - I'd better give it to Pat."

Pat met her round the next corner.

"Morning! Parcel for you! Sorry I'm a bit late!"

"And I have one for you!" said Miss Hubbard. "I found it lying in the street."

"Dear me, Miss Hubbard, I must have dropped it. Thank you! My bag is so full today!"

"Goodness me, Pat, I hope you'll take more care. It's taken a bit of a knock. And I don't think Mrs Crockett will be too pleased to get a *muddy* parcel."

"Now don't you worry, Miss Hubbard, I'll give it a wipe before I deliver it. It's very nice of you to pick it up for me. I've never seen so many parcels in all my days. It's a real worry, getting round the village with them. I can't use the van in these narrow yards, you know."

Pat went on his way.
"One thing - my bag gets lighter as I go along! Soon be done, now."
At last, his bag was empty.
"I'm glad that lot's finished!"

But, when he went back to the post office, there was another pile of parcels waiting for him.

"What's that? Not another load?"

"Oh, Pat, I'm so sorry," said Mrs Goggins. "I don't know where they're all coming from!"

"It's worse than Christmas!" said Pat. "What's going on? All the parcels in the world seem to be coming to Greendale!"

"Just take as many as you can," said Mrs Goggins, "then come back for another lot. That's the only way! Little by little - you'll manage."

"This bag's such a weight - it's giving me a sore back, and I need arms like a gorilla!"

There were so many parcels in Pat's van that there was hardly any room for Jess.

"Now then, Jess, where are you going to sit? Shove up a bit, and make room for another parcel. One of these days, there won't be enough room for *me* to get in," said Pat, "then *you'll* have to drive the van, Jess!"

Pat squeezed in somehow, and went on his way.

The first stop today was
Thompson Ground.
Sam's van was ahead of Pat,
and there was Dorothy,
looking at a big glossy catalogue,
full of coloured pictures.

There was a pile of parcels for her.
"Now, then, Dorothy," said Pat.
"Just look at this lot! All for you!"

"Oooh, Pat, how nice!" said Dorothy.
"I was hoping they'd come today."

"I can't say I was! I've had a
huge load of parcels today. It's like
ten Christmases all at once! Where
are they all coming from?"

"It's this here catalogue, Pat,"
said Sam. "It's got *everything* in!
All the things I can't fit into my van!
Folks love it! They're ordering
stuff like mad, and they all come
through the post."

"Now I see!" said Pat.
"Skirts and blouses!" said Dorothy.
"TVs and videos!" said Sam.
"Pots and pans!" said Dorothy.
"Oh, help!" said Pat.
"Cheerio!" said Sam.

Pat was on his way.

"Nay, Jess!" he said. "It's going to get worse. I don't know what we're going to do. It'll be beds and wardrobes, next."

At Ted Glen's, Ted was looking out for Pat. There was the biggest pile of parcels for Ted.

Pat staggered up to the door with them, dropping them as he went.
"Ooooops!"
"Hey up, Pat!" said Ted, as he caught the flying parcels.
"What this, then? A new sort of air-mail?"

"Sorry about that, Ted, but I just can't cope. Everybody's gone mad, ordering every mortal thing from that catalogue of Sam's."

"Well, you'll have to move with the times, Pat. Come up to date! It's no good staggering round with a bag of parcels, breaking your arm."

"I can't get the van round these lanes and yards in the villages," said Pat.

"Nay, Pat, you want a high-tech solution. I'll have a think about it. I'm sure I can come up with something."

"I hope you can," said Pat, "before I get squashed under a pile of parcels. Cheerio!"

The next day, Major Forbes was on the look-out for a parcel he had sent for, when he spotted Pat, behind a high pile of parcels!

"By Jove!" barked the Major, "there's my parcel, right at the bottom! I'll just –"

"Oh!!! Help!" yelled Pat, as the Major tugged his parcel out, making all the other parcels tumble to the ground.

"It's all right, Pat," said the Major, "I've got it! Bye bye!"

Round the corner, Doctor Gilbertson was chatting to Dorothy
Thompson . . .

". . . and I was just saying I could do with a new car, when
Sam showed me that catalogue of his."

"Ooh, yes, it's wonderful," said Dorothy. "There's everything in it."

Pat walked straight into Doctor Gilbertson, and his parcels went
flying again!

"Whoa!" he shouted.

"Oh, help!" said Dorothy. "What's —?"

Doctor Gilbertson helped Pat up and said,

"Now, Pat, you don't need to be so rough about delivering the mail!
I'll be having some broken legs to mend."

"I'm sorry, Doctor," said Pat. "It's this mail-order madness that's
come over the whole of Greendale."

"Well I think the Royal Mail should do something about it," said the
doctor. "It's not good for your health - or for ours, if it comes to that!
What if I order a new car? I'll put a word in with your boss, in Pencaster."

"Well, I hope somebody does something!" said Pat. "A new car? Now
that would make a super parcel! I don't think *that* would go in my bag."

The next day, it was time to call on Ted again.
He was too busy to look out for Pat.
"More parcels!"
"Have a look at this, Pat," said Ted.
"I think it'll solve your problem.
The Mark One, Super Speed,
Postal Scooter! Just what the modern
postman needs in the age of mail-order!"
"It looks grand, Ted.
I like the parcel-box in front.
Is there room for a cat?"
"There's room for everything.
Why don't you try it out?
Have a test-run."
"Well, I don't know how you've
done it so quickly. I'll just try the seat.
What are you doing, Ted?
You're not starting the engine are you?
How do you turn it off?"

But Pat's question
was too late.
The Postal Scooter
shot out of the workshop
door, taking Pat with it.
"Ohhhhhh!"

Pat shot down the hill, through an open gate, into a field,
and crashed into a haystack.

"Are you all right, Pat?" panted Ted, when he found Pat. "I think
it needs a bit of fettling before you use it for real, a few adjustments . . ."

"Ermm - yes, Ted, quite a few," said Pat, picking himself out of
the hay. "Like, well, putting brakes on it?"

A few days later, Mrs Pottage was talking to Mrs Goggins outside the post office . . .

"That Pat, he makes a great racket, these days, when he goes round with the village post."

"Aye, well, it is a bit noisy," said Mrs Goggins, "but he certainly gets round with the parcels, now."

"But he seems to think he's in some sort of race!" said Mrs Pottage.

There was a loud bang, and Pat came whizzing along the village street on his Postal Scooter.

Mrs Goggins and Mrs Pottage jumped into the post office doorway for safety.

"I see what you mean!" said Mrs Goggins.

PC Selby was having a quiet stroll, when Pat shot into view. He jumped into Mr Pringle's garden. Pat shot in at the open gate, and out the other end.

"My goodness," said Mr Pringle, "Pat *is* in a hurry! Must be a terribly urgent telegram - but why did he come through here?"

The steep hills slowed Pat down a bit, but only when he was going *up* them!
Pat tumbled off at the bottom of one hill, with parcels scattered all about.
George Lancaster came along and helped to gather them up,
saying, "Here you are Pat. Are you trying to sow them?"

PC Selby was looking for Pat in the post office.

"Morning, Mrs Goggins. Can I have a quiet word?" he said.

"I thought you might be popping in," said Mrs Goggins.

"I've had complaints. It's this high-speed postman of ours."

"Poor old Pat," said Mrs Goggins. "He's only trying to do his job."

"Right enough, but he's making a dickens of a racket, and endangering life and limb."

"Let me have a word with Pat," said Mrs Goggins. "I know he'll listen to me. No need for him to be in trouble."

"I'll leave it to you, then," said PC Selby. "A word to the wise, eh? Thanks. See you, Mrs Goggins !"

Pat came in, a minute later.

"Was that PC Selby just now?" he said.

"Yes, it was, Pat, and it was you he was talking about. He's taken your name and address."

"He knows it! We went to school together."

"Never mind that. He's really cross with you. Been causing a lot of noise and danger, haven't you? Tearing round on that scooter-thing!"

"But - how else can I deliver all the parcels on time, if they keep on coming like this?"

"Well, Pat, just as it happens, there's a parcel for *you* today - it's a big one; have a look in it, you never know what it might be."

"For me? Well - who can be sending one for me? I certainly haven't ordered anything from that blooming catalogue."

Pat unwrapped the huge parcel.

"Well, bless me - it's - it's - one of those trolleys - a proper postal-trolley - I saw one when I went to London on that trip! Well, this should be a bit of all right. Let's get it loaded up . . ."

Off Pat went, proudly wheeling his postal-trolley.
He met the Reverend Timms.
"What do you reckon to this, Reverend?" said Pat.
"Wonderful! Ah, Pat, you see, the Lord will provide."
"No, it came from the Royal Mail in Pencaster,"
said Pat. "It's to help me deal with all these parcels."
"And it's nice and quiet,"
said the Reverend Timms.
"Just the thing for our peaceful
corner of the world. Bye, Pat!"

Doctor Gilbertson was out shopping.
"Morning, Doctor Gilbertson!"
"Hello, Pat. I like your
new trolley! Nice and
quiet. Holds more
parcels, too."
"It'll save me
going off *my*
trolley," said
Pat, "I can
tell you!"

Pat went, whistling cheerfully, up the village street. Jess rode
amongst the parcels and packets; he loved it. "Come on, Jess," said Pat.
"You can give *me* a ride when we've done."

But Jess wasn't at all sure about that. Who ever heard of a cat pulling a trolley?

Postman Pat™

and the big surprise

It was a lovely morning in Greendale. The flowers were blooming in Pat's garden, and so were the weeds! Pat was up early. There might be time to do a spot of weeding before he went to work.

"Now then," said Pat, "where did I put that spade? Here we are! Just the job. This'll soon get rid of those bloomin' weeds."

Sara was looking at the clock in the kitchen. "Just look at that time, Pat's going to be late with the post. Pat! You'd best leave your gardening, now! Time's getting on; it's nearly quarter past!"

"Hang on!" said Pat. "I'll be there in a minute! I'll just shift this..."
Pat was pulling at a big clump of grass.
"Out you come! One... two... three! Heave ho - hup! OUCH!!! Oh, dear! Oh, help... owwwwohhhh! Oh, my poor old back! Oh, Sara!"

"Whatever's wrong, Pat?" shouted Sara.
"Oh, deary me, what's happened to you?"
"It's my back," said Pat.
"It doesn't half hurt!
I was just pulling this grass!"

"Here, let me just straighten you up," said Sara.

"OWWWWWW! Oh, stop, it's worse like that!"

Sara didn't know what to do.

"Oh, I think I'd better call the doctor," she said, "I can't leave you standing there all day, propped up on the table."

What luck! There was Doctor Gilbertson passing the window. Sara waved to the Doctor, and ran out to speak to her.

"What a piece of luck, Doctor, seeing you! Poor old Pat's hurt his back, and he can't move a step! Can you come in and have a look at him?"

"Of course I can," said Doctor Gilbertson. "Poor Pat, we can't do with having our postman out of action!"

Sara was on her way.

Jess didn't know what was going on! He stayed at home, to keep Pat company, and cheer him up.

What a surprise Mrs Goggins had when the post-office door pinged, and in walked Sara!

"Morning, Mrs Goggins!"

"Morning, Pat," said Mrs Goggins. "Oh - hello - what's happened to - oh, it's Sara! Where's Pat?"

"He's hurt his back," said Sara, "and has to stay in bed. I'm taking the post today! It's all arranged with Pencaster."

"Oh, well, that's all right, then," said Mrs Goggins. "But poor old Pat, with a sore back, all laid up! But it'll be a nice change for you. Well, I hope you like it!"

"Oh, I'm sure I will," said Sara. "I'll manage all right."

"Could you just ask Dorothy Thompson for her carrot-cake recipe," said Mrs Goggins. "She promised it last week, and Pat forgot."

"Don't worry, I'll get it for you. Cheerio!"

Sara was singing as she went on her way, "Early in the morning . . ."

She met PC Selby.

"Morning Pa - oh, what - well, I'll be - is it Sara? Whatever are you doing with the post?"

"Pat's laid up with a bad back."

"Poor fellow. I had that once. It does hurt, an' all. Now, don't you worry about him. He'll soon be better. I'll pop in and see him later on - cheer him up a bit, like. Thanks for the letters! Bye!"

Sara's next stop was at the village church.

"Hello, anybody there? Morning, Reverend!"

"Bless me," said the Reverend Timms. "What's happened to your voice, Pat? Oh, it isn't Pat! Is it you, Sara? What a surprise! And a parcel! Lovely! But where is Pat?"

"Laid up with a bad back for the day!"

"Oh, the poor boy!" said the Reverend Timms. "I'll pop in and give him a game of chess; that'll take his mind off it. And I'll tell him how well you're getting on with the post."

"Thanks, Reverend! Cheerio!"

Sara was on her way.

At Thompson Ground, Dorothy Thompson was doing a
special baking.

"That sounds like Pat," she said. "Now, I wonder if he's forgotten?
It'll be a nice surprise. Morning, Pat, I just thought you - oh, it's Sara!"

"Yes, Pat's in bed with a bad back, so I'm doing the post instead - there are lots of letters for you, Dorothy."

"Pat, with a bad back? Today, of all days?"

"Well, what's so special about today?"

"Oh, you just wait and see, that's all! Only, you'd better be on your way, with all those letters to deliver. I'll not hold you up. Besides, I've been too busy to put the kettle on this morning."

"Oh, yes, well, I'll be off, then. Goodbye!"

"Well, what's she in such a hurry for?" Sara said to herself. "I'm sure Pat said she always gave him a cup of tea!"

When Sara called on Alf Thompson, he was walking across the yard with a large parcel. All he said was, "Hello Pat, I mean Sara, er, I'll just..." then he dodged into the barn, and she never saw him again.

"What *is* going on here?" said Sara. "Folks are acting a bit peculiar. I wonder if they're always like this? I must ask Pat."

Sara was on her way.

There was something going on at Granny Dryden's cottage, as well. Granny Dryden was trying on her best hat. Sara had a postcard for her.

"Oh, that must be Pat with the post!" said Granny Dryden.

"Morning, Granny Dryden!" said Sara. "There's a card for you!"

"Goodness gracious, what are you doing with the post, Sara? Have you done a job-swap, or whatever they call it?"

"Well, we have in a way; only Pat isn't doing any job today, apart from lying in bed with a bad back."

"A bad back? I had one once - before your time."

"I like your hat."

"I'm only trying it on to see if it fits," said Granny Dryden.

"Is it new?"

"Well, um, no, yes, that is, no, it's a bit parky today... It's just to keep me warm, like, well, um, you know what I mean. But I mustn't hold you back with all these letters to deliver. You'll be wanting to get back to see how Pat's getting on. Give him my love."

"Yes, I'll be off, then. Bye, Granny Dryden!"

"Everybody's rushing me on my way," Sara said. "No time for a chat. Well, perhaps they'd rather have Pat for their postman, after all!"

Sara went all day, up and down the winding roads, delivering letters and parcels to the people of Greendale. At last, it was time to head for home. She was looking forward to telling Pat all the doings of the day. What a strange day it had been! And how had Pat been getting on?

There was Jess, looking out for Sara on the doorstep.
"Hello, Jess! Have you been taking good care of Pat?"

Sara called up the stairs.
"Hello, Pat! I'm home! Are you still in bed?"

There was no answer. Where could he be?
"It's me... Sara!"
There was still no reply. Perhaps he's watching TV?
Then the door flew open, and . . .

. . . a chorus of voices sang out: "HAPPY ANNIVERSARY!"

"Anniversary? I thought everyone had forgotten - did Pat remember, after all?"

"With a little help from his friends!" said Granny Dryden. "We all wanted you to have a special party, as a big surprise. And the Doctor says Pat's back is almost better, so he can join in."

"And your hat?"

"Yes, it almost gave the surprise away, didn't it," said Granny Dryden, "when you caught me trying it on."

"Have a slice of Anniversary Cake!" said Dorothy Thompson. "I can
tell you, I had a shock when I saw you coming with the post. You
almost discovered the surprise!"

"Well, I did smell baking, but you didn't give me time to ask about it."

"But you haven't finished the day's post, Sara!" said Pat.
"I surely have!"
"No, there's one more parcel, and it's for you, Sara! Happy Anniversary, and thanks for everything, and for being such a marvellous wife."

"But that *isn't* the last parcel. There's another in the bottom of my bag! *This* one is for you, Pat! Happy Anniversary to you as well, and thanks for being such a marvellous husband!"

"And all our good wishes to two super post-people!" said Doctor Gilbertson. "Let's all drink to the happy couple. Here's to Sara and Pat!"

"Three cheers for everyone!" said Pat.
"Thanks for a lovely surprise party!"

Postman Pat™

and the hole in the road

It was a fine day in Greendale. Pat was on his way with his van full of letters and parcels for the village, and for the farms and cottages scattered all along the valley.

Down at Greendale village school they had made a model volcano.

"Just think, children," said Mr Pringle, "of all that hot rock going bubble, bubble, whoosh, under the ground!"

"You'd get your feet hot," said Katy.

"No you wouldn't," said Bill Thompson, sploshing away at his volcano painting. "You could wear your wellies."

"It was a long time before wellies were invented," said Mr Pringle. "The volcanoes made our lovely Greendale hills long before there were any people, never mind wellies. Great holes in the ground, with rock oozing out like toffee."

"Did you say toffee?" said Tom. "I like toffee."

"I said the rock was *like* toffee," said Mr Pringle, "because it was all oozy; and it was so long ago that it was even before the dinosaurs came. You can all do a lovely painting, tomorrow, for open day. But it's home-time, now!"

"What if . . ." said Julian, as they were putting their shoes on.
"What if there was a volcano under the ground . . . here, under
our school . . .?"

"Better put your wellies on, and look where you're going!"
said Katy.

"*Ooooh!*" said Lucy.

Pat was waiting at the gate for Julian.
"Time to go home!" said Pat.

The next morning, it seemed very quiet in the village when Pat was on his way to collect the letters. When he arrived at the post office, Mrs Goggins was talking to someone on the telephone.

"Ooooh, yes, I certainly will . . . don't you worry now, it will be all right, I feel sure of that. Did you say it was near Thompson Ground? Deary me! What next? Yes, I'll tell him . . . I'll tell him to be really careful . . . Bye for now."

"What was all that about, Mrs Goggins? What have I got to be so careful about?" said Pat.

"Oh, dear, well, that was PC Selby," said Mrs Goggins. "He's in ever such a canfaddle. It seems that there's a great gaping hole in the middle of the road, near Thompson Ground, and he doesn't want anyone falling down it. He says it's big enough to swallow a cow!"

"Oh, I know what that means," said Pat. "ROAD CLOSED - DIVERSION - cones and bollards, and bits of plastic tape all over the place. How does he think I'm going to get through with all these letters and parcels?"

"What a business it is!" said Mrs Goggins.

"It must be these volcanoes wakening up again," said Pat. "Julian was on about it last night. They've been doing it at school . . . volcanoes and earthquakes, and such like; that's how Greendale was made in the first place!"

"Nay, Pat, it's only a hole in the road - don't get carried away!" said Mrs Goggins.

"Well, I can't post all these letters in a hole in the road, can I? Never mind, the post always gets through, somehow. Cheerio!"

Pat was still muttering to himself as he loaded up his van.
"What if a dinosaur came galloping out of that hole! You never know what might happen! I wonder if dinosaurs get letters? Now then, Jess, what did dinosaur-cats look like? I bet they ate some huge fish!"

Alf was out on his tractor . . .

Pat stopped for a chat.

"What do you reckon to this hole in the road, Alf?"

"What hole?" said Alf. "I've seen nothing. I've been ploughing this field since early on . . ."

"There's a great hole, just outside your house. PC Selby's shut the road off. There are notices all over - NO ROAD, KEEP OUT, DANGER."

"Oh dear," said Alf. "How am I going to get home? I'd best be off."

There was a parcel for Greendale Farm . . .

"Hello! Is there anybody in?"

"Hello, Pat!" said Mrs Pottage. "Oooh, a lovely parcel!"

"Come and see our pictures," said Katy. "They're for our volcano project."

"Volcanoes?" said Pat. "You don't think it's a volcano making that great hole in the road, do you?"

"Oh, Pat, I don't think it can be as bad as all that!" said Mrs Pottage.

"I hope not," said Pat. "Cheerio! And mind how you go!"

Pat kept a careful look-out, just in case there were any new holes that no one knew about. When he came to the crossroads, he had to stop. There was a huge sign, with one word on it - DIVERSION - blocking the road ahead.

"Oh dear," said Pat. "We can't go that way!"
There was a blue arrow showing the new route, and Pat had to follow it.

"Now, Jess, where are we going to get to? I know Selby and his diversions. Last time I went this way— Hang on, I think we're lost . . ."

There was another DIVERSION sign blocking the road, with more blue arrows.

"Not another! But these arrows are pointing back the other way!"

Pat drove down a winding road. There was only just enough room for his van to squeeze between the hedges. Then he came to yet another DIVERSION!

"What's this? The man must be mad!" said Pat. "Oh, NO!
We *are* lost now. I think we're in Timbuctoo!"
    Jess wondered if there were any mice in Timbuctoo.
    "Now then . . . if we turn right here . . ." said Pat.
    But it was no good, it only led to another DIVERSION sign.
    Then Pat rubbed his eyes. "I've just spotted where we are, Jess!
We're back where we started!"

Then Alf came chugging along on his tractor.

"Don't follow me," said Pat. "I'm lost. If you follow these signs you just go round in a great big circle."

"Nay, Pat, I can't be bothered with all that," said Alf. "I have to get home and get my dinner. Let's shift this clutter out of the way."

Alf dumped the DIVERSION sign in the hedge.
"There you are, no problem!" said Alf, and he drove off down the road. Pat followed not far behind.

Near to Thompson Ground there were red cones and plastic tapes, flashing lights and notices all over the road. In the middle of all this, there was a small hole.

"Is that what all this fuss has been about?" said Alf. "It doesn't look much to me."

"It must be a mini volcano," said Pat.

"A baby one," said Alf. "I reckon Ted could fill that in, no bother. Look out! Here comes trouble!"

PC Selby was coming towards them with a cup of tea in one hand.

"Now then, now then, what's going on here?" he said, in his special policeman's voice. "Come on, lads, you know this road's closed, you must have seen the signs. It's my duty to warn you . . . and I'll have to take your names and addresses . . ."

"Don't be daft, Arthur," said Pat. "You've known us ever since we were in short trousers."

"Never mind that," said PC Selby, "we have to do it proper. Can you just hold my tea? Now then, how do you spell 'proceeding'? Watch that tea . . . You haven't got a pencil-sharpener on you, by any chance? Come here, let's have a sup before it goes cold . . ."

Now Dorothy came out with a pot of tea and cups and saucers on a tray.

"Here we are, a nice fresh cup of tea - and a top-up for Arthur - that'll buck everybody up . . ."

"Ooh, thanks, Dorothy," said Pat. "Just what we need. Two sugars, Arthur?"

"And three for me," said Alf. "Dorothy, have you got anything to sharpen Arthur's pencil? I'll hold your tea— Hang on, Pat, if you could just hold this . . . and then, Arthur, pass your pencil to Dorothy, then if you can hold this . . ."

They didn't seem to have enough hands to hold all the cups of tea, and the pencil, and the notebook, and the pencil-sharpener.

They juggled all these things between them.

"OOPS!" said Alf. "Look out, you're slopping my tea!"

"I think there are two 'e's' in proceeding," said Pat. "But is it a 'c' or an 's'? Watch that tea!"

"Ermm . . . has anyone seen my notebook?" said PC Selby.

"I think it's going round in circles, like my van!" said Pat. "It's sure to come back to where it started."

"Talking about that," said PC Selby, "you've given me an idea. Now then, if we made all the traffic go through Alf's yard, instead . . ."

Pat gave Dorothy her letters, and left them to discuss the new plan.

He still had a lot of letters to deliver.

When he called on Miss Hubbard she was acting very oddly - prodding about the garden with her stick.

"Oh! Morning, Pat!" she said.

"Morning, Miss Hubbard. You've not lost that ring again, have you?"

"Certainly not! I'm just taking precautions . . . holes, you know, appearing without warning. You never know what's going on these days . . . PC Selby told me all about it - volcanoes, earthquakes . . . it's these new-fangled things doing it, all these objects whizzing about in the sky . . . flying saucers . . . who can tell?"

"Oh, I wouldn't let it bother you, Miss Hubbard," said Pat.
"Just get your taters in, the way you always did, and nothing much'll
go wrong. Cheerio!"

Pat called on Ted Glen. There was a parcel for him.

"Sorry I'm a bit late today," said Pat. "It's this hole in the road - I've had to go all round Greendale to get here."

"Don't worry," said Ted. "Leave it to me. I'll have that hole filled in in no time - a bag of sand and cement, and plenty of gravel and tar - that'll sort it out. All that lot was left over from fettling that old house in Pencaster - I knew it would come in handy one day."

"Champion," said Pat.

Pat was on his way.

George Lancaster was busy sorting his eggs . . .

"Morning, George! My goodness, you have a lot of letters today!"

"It's my birthday!" said George, smiling.

"Happy Birthday, George!" said Pat. "You'll find a special one from me and Sara, somewhere among that lot! Cheerio!"

Pat had delivered all his letters. It was time to go back to the post office, to see if any more letters had come in from Pencaster. He stopped at Thompson Ground to see how things were going. There was a whole new set of signs, leading into the field and through Alf's yard where Ted's lorry was parked.

"It's like town centre here," said Alf. "My poor hens - they're all mizzled, poor things - don't know which way from t'other - they'll not lay for a fortnight. Here comes another van . . . oh, it's Sam!"

Sam Waldron drove through in his mobile shop, tooting his horn.

"See what I mean, Pat? It's terrible!"

"You'll be all right," said Pat, "as soon as Ted gets that hole filled in."

PC Selby stood in the middle of the road, directing the traffic.

"Come on! Slowly as you go! Careful, now! Watch these hens!"

"Tea up!" called Dorothy, from the kitchen door. "And fresh biscuits, straight from the oven!"

"Just what I need," said Ted. "We'll have a sup while that tar sets. Are you coming for your tea, Arthur?"

Something seemed to be keeping PC Selby!

"Help!"

"Did somebody shout 'Help'?" said Pat.

"He's not still looking for his notebook, is he?" said Alf.

"We'd better go and see what's up," said Ted.

There was PC Selby, in the middle of the road, stuck fast! Ted
looked closely at his big police boots.

"What are you doing to my nice new tar?" said Ted. "Fast-setting
stuff, that - a new kind, you know."

"I've brought you a nice cup of tea," said Alf, "till we can get you
unstuck . . ."

"You'll have to take your boots off and leave them in charge," said Pat. "It's a good thing there isn't a volcano under there!"

So PC Selby loosened his boots, and Alf brought a wheelbarrow to wheel him to the house.

"Time for a bit of farm transport," said Alf.

"We'll need a new warning-sign," said Pat.

He found a big piece of card in his van, and wrote on it with his felt-pen:

"There - everybody should see that," said Pat. "And that's quite enough of volcanoes, for one day. I hope Dorothy's kept that tea hot!"